The Long, Long Line

Tomoko Ohmura

Welcome! This is the end of the line.
PLEASE LINE UP IN SINGLE FILE.
#50
Frog

I can't wait.
Me neither!
A one and a two and...
It's so popular!
It always is.
#49 Lizard
#48 Mouse
#47 Mole
#46 Flying Squirrel
#45 Squirrel
#44 Turtle
#43 Guinea Pig

Please line up in order!

What's this line for?
What? You don't know?
It stinks!
Oops! Sorry...
#42 Weasel
#41 Hedgehog
#40 Rabbit
#39 Armadillo
#38 Skunk
#37 Porcupine

#36
Cat

#35
Monkey

#34
Dog

#33
Raccoon

You can't
beat me!
Go! Go! Go!
#32
Fox
#31
Otter
#30
Sloth
#29
Koala

Give me some room.
There's space up there.
Move up a bit more!
I'm trying...
#28 Beaver
#27 Chimpanzee
#26 Orangutan
#25 Goat
#24 Pig

#23
Sheep

Looks tasty...
Oh dear...
#22
Wolf
#21
Wombat
#20
Boar

Hang in there just a bit longer!
Are we there yet?
Peek-a-boo!
#19
Kangaroo
#18
Hyena

#17
Panda

#16
Cow

Gorilla!
A... Apple.
#15
Deer
#14
Gorilla

#13
Leopard

#12
Tapir

Pink.
Knob.
Bird!
Oh no—I lose!
#11
Seal
#10
Bear

I'm hungry!
ROAR!
H-here's some seaweed, if you like.
#9
Lion
#8
Zebra

Give me some, too!
#7
Tiger

Yaaaawn!
How much longer
will it be?
#6
Camel

You're almost there!
Ahhhhh...
Now I'm yawning,
too!
#5
Crocodile

#4
Hippopotamus

Charge!
#3
Rhinoceros

Finally, it's our turn!
#2
Giraffe

Here we go!

J U M B O

YAAA

Thank you for waiting, and welcome aboard! One at a time, please!
#1
Elephant

First, the Whale Somersault!
One!

AAAY!

C
O
A
S
T
E
R

Two!
And three!

Glub glub glub

Next, the Whale Dive!
And finally...

SPL

...the Whale Water Spray!!
ASH!

And we're

done!
That felt good!
I'm getting back in line!
Watch your step!

Looks like that's it for today! Let's come back again sometime.

Today's Riders

1. Elephant
2. Giraffe
3. Rhinoceros
4. Hippopotamus
5. Crocodile
6. Camel
7. Tiger
8. Zebra
9. Lion
10. Bear
11. Seal
12. Tapir
13. Leopard
14. Gorilla
15. Deer
16. Cow
17. Panda
18. Hyena
19. Kangaroo
20. Boar
21. Wombat
22. Wolf
23. Sheep
24. Pig
25. Goat
26. Orangutan
27. Chimpanzee
28. Beaver
29. Koala
30. Sloth
31. Otter
32. Fox
33. Raccoon
34. Dog
35. Monkey
36. Cat
37. Porcupine
38. Skunk
39. Armadillo
40. Rabbit
41. Hedgehog
42. Weasel
43. Guinea Pig
44. Turtle
45. Squirrel
46. Flying Squirrel
47. Mole
48. Mouse
49. Lizard
50. Frog

Ride operator: Whale
Ride guide: Bird

Published in North America in 2013 by Owlkids Books Inc.

Published in Japan under the title *Nanno Gyôretsu?* in 2009 by Poplar Publishing Co., Ltd., Tokyo.

English Translation rights arranged with Poplar Publishing Co., Ltd., through Japan Foreign-Rights Centre

Owlkids Books acknowledges the financial support of the Canada Council for the Arts, the Ontario Arts Council, the Government of Canada through the Canada Book Fund (CBF) and the Government of Ontario through the Ontario Media Development Corporation's Book Initiative for our publishing activities.

Published in Canada by
Owlkids Books Inc.
10 Lower Spadina Avenue
Toronto, ON M5V 2Z2

Published in the United States by
Owlkids Books Inc.
1700 Fourth Street
Berkeley, CA 94710

Library and Archives Canada Cataloguing in Publication

Ohmura, Tomoko
The long, long line / Tomoko Ohmura.

Translation of: Nanno Gyo^retsu.
ISBN 978-1-926973-92-0

I. Title.

PZ7.O46Lo 2013 j895.6'36 C2012-908547-2

Library of Congress Control Number: 2013930499

Manufactured in Shenzhen, Guangdong, China, in September 2013, by WKT Co. Ltd.
Job #13CB1617

B C D E F G

Publisher of Chirp, chickaDEE and OWL
www.owlkidsbooks.com